The Power of Love

Dieudonné

Can two people from different continents and cultures fall in love by communicating through writing?

Freddy Daix

Contents

Dieudonné

This book is about something special which is more valuable than gold and diamond, and still with all the money in the world one cannot buy it. Because we all have it within ourselves for it is the essence of life, and the reason why we need one another to be complete. It's called love.

Love for our family, love for our friends, and love for the one special person that we meet one day somewhere in life and with whom we fall in love. We will leave our family and friends to be with that person without fear, but feeling secure and happy. And for the first time in our lives, we will be willing to spend the rest of our days together as a couple, walking side by side and holding hands on the road of love until death do us apart.

Love is the most beautiful and powerful thing that comes to us freely, that will make the impossible a reality by conquering any obstacles. Love will even travel between continents and culture to find its other half.

How does love sometimes come to us without our knowledge? Can two people from different continents with different cultures fall in love just by communicating through writing? The answer is yes. Only if their love is powerful enough to see beyond the boundaries of their own eyes.

Chapter 1

Bouaké was my home, the city where I grew up and went to school. It was the second largest city after Abidjan, the capital, and was in the center of my beautiful country, Côte d'Ivoire. The location of Bouaké made it good for trade and business, and with its people from diverse backgrounds coming from every part of Africa, and the rest of the world, that also made Bouaké a cosmopolitan city. The downtown area where all the activities and businesses were located was called, Le Commerce, translated in English means the Shopping Center.

You could walk around all of downtown in less than an hour, as everything was within walking distance. And you could also see downtown Main Street shops and businesses on every corner with one of its most popular clothing stores called Novafric. It was the store where everyone who dreamed of the latest fashion clothes would go shopping. Down the street from the store was a popular driving school, Paris Auto Ecole, and a couple blocks away was a beautiful and big four-star hotel, Hotel

Harmattan, where only the rich and famous stayed. And not too far from the stop light was the main post office, and right across the street was another beautiful four-star hotel, Ran Hotel, next to the train station. All of these were the main attractions of downtown Bouaké.

Bouaké by night was about eating and drinking with friends. But for people that were looking to party, they would go to the most popular night club, Le Savannah.

Bouaké was also known for its public zoo where you would find different kinds of animals, and about ten minutes' drive from the zoo was its famous public swimming pool, La Piscine Municipale. People would travel from every part of the country to visit the zoo, and later enjoy the nice weather with a cold drink at the bar by the poolside.

But Bouaké was most known for its fair and carnival which happened once a year in the spring. It was called, La Semaine Commerciale, which means the shopping week. The fair was a major attraction for the city, it lasted for two weeks and was twenty-four hours a day nonstop. It was a place for big and small businesses to market themselves, and a place to meet old friends and make new friends. During the day, the fair was a marketplace for bargain shoppers, music listeners and good food. At night it was all about partying, drinking, and eating in a typical African restaurant called, Maquis.

At the end of the two-week fair, the last Saturday was the election of Miss Carnival. So, every girl came from different parts of the country days before to participate in the pre-selection of Miss Carnival, where the most beautiful girl of the night was chosen from among them by a jury panel. The girls came not only for the beauty contest, but also for the prizes and the job opportunities that came with winning Miss Carnival. The pageant took place at the public swimming pool decorated with colorful lights, balloons and different artists playing with a band all night which made the night very special.

Everybody would be sitting at home in front of their TV screen watching the pageant with excitement to see who the new Miss Carnival would be. At the end of the night after the new Miss Carnival was crowned, it was all celebrated with a masked party dance, called le Bal Masqué, where every man and woman on the dance floor wore a mask of their choice.

But the best was still yet to come, the Carnival Parade.

The following day, Sunday from two o'clock in the afternoon to six o'clock pm, was the Carnival Parade to close the festival. Men, women, and children would stand by the roadside to watch the parade of different groups with colorful costumes go by. And for most of us to see up close for the first time the new Miss Carnival. She would be standing on a flatbed of a cargo truck with the two runner ups each by her side, and all three wearing a sexy swimsuit turning side by side to the spectators to show their beautiful silhouettes as they drove by. At the end of the parade, the best costume was voted on for a prize, and Papa Carnival was burned down to close the carnival.

But above everything, what made Bouaké so special and dear to my heart was its people and the lifestyle. The people were kind and friendly and always open for a conversation. Life was nice and simple and not as active as Abidjan the capital, which made Bouaké an attractive city for people to visit and spend the weekend.

Chapter 2

It was ten o'clock Friday morning, the sun was bright and shining as always in my country. It was a beautiful day and like on every campus, Friday was always a special day for all students. As the last day of the school week and the beginning of the weekend, Friday night was a night full of drinks, girls, and good times with friends in bars and maquis.

A student with money on campus Friday night was the man of the hour, because he was able to buy the drinks, the food and even make a small loan to a friend. And although money was important for a successful party, people in Africa knew how to have a good time with the little money they had. We learned to maximize a good time by sharing together what each person brought to the table. And a party in Africa really meant to party because it lasted until the early morning.

As I stood alone with my back against the school wall, I was thinking of everything that morning, but Friday night parties. I was dreaming of something totally different from others. All I wanted was a letter, an envelope with my name on it would have made my day. I had been checking my mailbox on campus for the last six weeks, always optimistic about getting a letter, only to return to class empty handed each time.

Unlike other students, I wasn't expecting a letter from my parents. I lived on campus and visited my parents every weekend in the same city. It was my last semester, and I was soon to graduate with a master's degree in Business. So ahead of me was a life full of ambition and good times, still all I could think about was someone special to me, and dear to my heart. Her name was Sharon Johnson, she was my pen pal and my best friend. We met through a Pen Pal agency via a P.O. Box, and because I didn't own a computer, the only way we could communicate was through writing.

Although I prayed for that morning to be different from the past weeks, I still walked to my mailbox with less optimism than the day before, maybe because I didn't know how she really felt about me, or I was just afraid to lose her friendship by her silence. I guess, I was desperate to read a letter from my friend.

So, what a wonderful surprise it was when I looked in my mailbox and saw an envelope flipped on the back. And without even reading the sender's name in the left corner, I folded the envelope in half and put it in the front pocket of my shirt, and as if I was looking for somewhere more secure to hide it, I took the letter out to put it in the back pocket of my pants and closed the button flap. I knew the letter was from Sharon by the stamp on the envelope which I had a glance of while folding it. But for some reason after waiting so long for her response, I was too excited to read the letter right away.

As I was walking down the stairs happy and impatient with my letter secured in my back pocket, I tripped, twisted my ankle, and almost fell on my face. I was only able to retain my balance by holding tight to the stair rails. A bit embarrassed and still in pain, I tried to walk as normally as I could in front of the students standing by. I stretched my leg a couple times along the way and tried to walk faster, but I still could hear the laughter and voices of the students, so I sped up my footsteps and took the first turn behind a building.

Then suddenly as if nothing had happened, everything was quiet, and I was all alone. At first, I was a little bit disoriented and out of place for a second. I looked back to make sure I wasn't followed, before looking around to familiarize myself with my own campus and look for a seat to recover from my ankle pain.

I found a flat surface under a tree, wiped the leaves off the ground between the roots with my hand and sat down. And with my knee bent I tried to massage my ankle, then turned my foot left and right to make sure everything was okay. I then took out my letter from my pocket and kissed the front of the envelope for good luck before opening it.

After I read the first paragraph, like a miracle, my ankle pain was gone. Because no pain was greater than the joy I felt. I read the letter once, twice, and still in disbelief, I read it again the third time slowly and out loud to hear each word through my ears to make sure I wasn't dreaming. Because the answer that I had been waiting for, all through our friendship was now in my hand on a piece of paper.

New York, June 5th

Dear Dieudonné,

It is almost summer in New York, the flowers are as colorful as the weather is beautiful, and it's about seventy-five degrees outside. I can see people walking and running in Central Park and enjoying the weather. That's why I love New York so much, the land of opportunity and the city of life. Someone might say, this is the best time to visit New York. But as much as this might sound crazy to you as it is to me, just the thought of it there is no other place I would rather be now than in Africa with you.

I'm writing my thesis for my master's degree about African culture. So, I decided to go to Africa for the first time to do my research, and finally meet you. I think you being from Africa and by my side will help me a lot with my research and the translation. I also wanted to meet you because after more than a year of friendship, each time that I wrote to you, I felt something deeper, a feeling that I seem unable to overcome unless I see you in person to know what it really is.

Although we have not seen a photo of each other, I fell in love with your style of writing. I read all your letters each time more than once, your sweet and soft words of compassion touched my heart. Your letters are romantic and passionate, therefore, to find the answer to my own feelings and know who you are, I decided to come to your country for my research.

I spoke to my parents about you and my trip to Africa for my research and got their support, and I also went to the embassy of Cote d'Ivoire in Washington DC, for my visa and received all the information needed including the hotels. I will be flying from JFK International Airport on July 1st and should be in Bouake July 2nd at 10:30 am. I look forward to meeting you and your family. I know this might come as a big surprise, but I hope you are as excited to see me as I am to see you.

See you soon kisses,

Sharon

A few minutes earlier I was worrying about not knowing her feelings for me and the fear of losing her friendship. Now to my surprise, she was coming to Africa to look for the same answer as me. Her timing to visit Africa couldn't have been better, because July 1st was the first day of the summer break.

That Friday morning became the best day of my semester, and for the first time in a long time I was also looking forward to a wonderful summer break. But it was still hard for me to believe that after writing to each other for a little more than a year, we would finally be meeting for the first time in a few weeks. I was now wondering what she might look like and what she would think of me. Would I be able to recognize her at the airport when she arrived? How tall was she? Her face? So many questions to which I had no answer for. Because at the beginning of our correspondence for some reason known only to her, she decided that we wouldn't exchange a photo, so we could avoid being judgmental of our appearance.

Instead, she wanted to wait and see how far our new friendship would take us first through our writing. And from that moment on, I knew there was something special about her, but I was also a bit skeptical and thought that maybe she was hiding something about her own appearance. But while she was looking for someone to connect with to build a true friendship, all I wanted at that time was just a pen pal, someone to write to.

At first, I thought it was impossible to write to her without having any idea what she looked like and that I would be unable to give her any compliment. I believed the correspondence wouldn't last, but eventually decided to give it a try anyway. Then I quickly realized the more curious I was about knowing her, the more I found myself writing to her and soon her picture didn't matter anymore. And as time went on, we found a true connection through our writing and learned more about things we like and dislike.

So, choosing not to exchange any photo had its benefits. It gave us the chance to know each other better and appreciate our friendship more. Her letters were optimistic, making me believe that anything was possible in life if you truly believe in yourself.

I learned through our friendship that true love was blind to physical beauty, but one could still feel it in his heart with his eyes closed. It's the love that is strong enough to bring two people close together even without seeing each other, no matter how far apart they may be. So, I was excited and looking forward to meeting her, but at the same time I was also scared because I didn't know how she would react when she saw me for the first time.

I went home earlier than usual that Friday afternoon to share the good news with my parents. Both my parents were teachers, my father was a high school math teacher and my mother a middle school French teacher. I had always admired my father growing up, and I wished to be like him one day. He was always optimistic about life no matter the circumstances. He taught me how important education was to be successful in life, and why even if a college degree didn't guarantee the best job, still the knowledge I would acquire through college will teach me innovative thinking and problem solving.

My mother was also a loving and caring woman, she was always willing to help others in need. She taught me that something good would always come from a positive attitude and being respectful toward others no matter their age would carry me a long way in life. I believed their compassion and caring attitude came from their teaching background that made them wonderful parents, and me a lucky son to have them in my life.

My parents owned a single-family home, it was a beautiful and modest sized house with three bedrooms. It had a living room, a dining room, and a kitchen. Next to the living room was a small office for my father. In front of the house there was a small yard with an attached one car garage. And in the back, there was a beautiful big backyard that my mother used for her gardening.

As I walked in the living room, I could see my father sitting at his desk grading his student's papers with the TV on. I also knew that my mother was cooking, because I could smell the sweet aroma of my favorite dish, peanut butter sauce, coming from the kitchen. The smell of peanut butter sauce and fresh habanero pepper was everywhere in the living room, which made me sneeze a couple times, and it felt like I could taste it on my lips. When it came to cooking, no one cooks better than my mother does although she was a teacher by profession.

After I said hello to my father, I asked my mother to join us in the living room and handed them the letter. They read the letter as I anxiously sat on the edge of the couch waiting for their reaction. Then, they both looked at me and smiled, so I knew they were happy for me to finally meet Sharon, because of how much I've talked about her.

"You still don't know what each other look like?" My father asked.

"No. It's what in the heart that counts, Dad". I replied smiling.

"I'm sure she is as beautiful as you are handsome". My mother said in support of me. And continued. "You should ask her to stay with us, she will be more than welcome in our house".

I replied to Sharon's letter the next day and told her that my parents and I welcome her with open arms in our house. I had a long list of things to do with her when she came to Africa, places to visit and things to see. I wanted to make sure she had access to all the research she needed for her thesis and had a good time. From that day on I went to school with a new attitude, and I was a new man in my own way. I felt special because I was expecting a visit from my best friend from America. A week later she replied to my letter to confirm again the date and time of her arrival and accepted the invitation to stay with us. My parents and I didn't waste any time to start getting the house ready.

Chapter 3

It was June 25th, finally the day had come to get the fruit of my education, days and sleepless nights of study had come to an end. It was graduation day; I was sitting among the graduate students dressed in my blue gown waiting for my name to be called.

As I heard my name, I walked to the podium to receive my master's degree and walking back to my seat I looked at my parents and saw tears of happiness coming down my mother's face, and the joy of a proud parent in my father's eyes. After the graduation ceremony, instead of having a big graduation party as planned months ago, we went to a restaurant with a few close friends for dinner. I had asked my parents days before to postpone my graduation party to coincide with Sharon's arrival a week later so that we could all celebrate together.

The weeks went by as fast as I could remember reading her last letter. School was now over; my parents and I were able to get everything done in time before Sharon's arrival. The whole house was cleaned and checked twice, her bedroom was nice and ready.

It was July 1st, the night before her arrival, I went to bed earlier than usual to be up on time the next morning for the long drive to the airport. And since her flight was arriving at 10:30am, I set my alarm clock for 6:30am to give my father enough time to be ready.

Then I closed my eyes and went to sleep, so I thought. But it didn't take me too long to realize it was going to be a different kind of night. After lying down on my bed for a few minutes with my pillow between my arm and my head, I tossed and turned around trying to find the best position. But I was unable to keep my eyes closed because I was still thinking of Sharon and what she might look like. For some strange reason my ears were still captured by the sound of each tick-tock of my alarm clock. So now here I was with my eyes wide open staring at the hands of the alarm clock, as I watched the second hand go around slowly moving the minute hand by one, and each time it seemed as if the hour hand had never moved.

A night without sleep seemed endless and the wait for morning to come was unbearable. But as the clock started to look bleary to my tired eyes, the sound of each "tick-tock" ironically became the perfect melody to my ears to finally put me to sleep. Until I jumped off my bed the next morning surprised by the loud alarm buzz. I knew it was going to be a beautiful day, because I could see the sunlight shining through a crack in my window and reflecting on my bedroom wall as if to say hello!

With my parents still sleeping, I went ahead brushed my teeth and took a shower. I put on my best clothes, a blue Polo t-shirt and a pair of Levi's jeans with my favorite Nike shoes. As the saying goes: "There is no second chance to make a first impression".

I wanted to look cool for Sharon, and make a good first impression, and I guess somewhere within me I wanted to look American. I was standing in front of the mirror practicing my speech for her when I heard a voice from behind me.

"Isn't it a little too early for the airport?" It was my father.

Surprised, I replied. "Just wanted to make sure we arrive at the airport on time".

At that precise moment I wished for one thing, that I was the one driving to the airport to pick up Sharon. But sadly, I didn't have a driver's license, nor did I know how to drive. My driving experience was only limited to the weekend when I was washing my father's car.

My father had a white four door Renault 4; it was a French made vehicle and one of the most popular cars in Africa, so every mechanic knew how to fix a Renault which made repairs cheaper. I looked forward to washing my father's car every Saturday morning, because it was the only time, I had to practice my driving skills a few feet away from the garage.

Each Saturday morning, I would sit in the driver's seat and turn the key to start the car. Then I would put the car in reverse to drive about thirty feet outside the garage. I knew exactly when and where to stop the car before putting the hand brake on, because I had been doing the same thing for so long that I knew it by heart.

And the best part was every time after I was done washing the car, I would do my usual routine before parking the car back in the garage. With the hand brake still on and the engine running, I would put my foot against the accelerator pedal to give it two or three pushes just to hear the amazing sound of the four cylinders engine. The last push was always the longest and loudest and gave a cranking noise to the engine which would call for my father's attention as he was expecting me to do so.

"It's not a race car Dieudonné!" He would always yell.

"I told you I was ready for my driver's license Dad". I would reply with a smile.

And the last push of the pedal made my day. Because I felt like a professional race car driver impatiently waiting for the race to start. But I understood why my father wanted me to wait until after college before getting a driver's license. He was just concerned with how many bad drivers were on the road and my safety.

"You will be more responsible and mature after college, and that will make you a good driver". He would always say.

A car has always been considered a luxury in Africa. The expense of buying a car and the added cost of routine maintenance with the high price of gas, made it a privilege for anyone to own a vehicle. But the cost of a driver's license made it even harder for anyone to learn how to drive. Because the price of a driver's license was more than most people's monthly salary.

The writing test alone was as hard as driving, so the chance of passing the driving test the first time was almost impossible, unless you bribed the driving instructor or were a very good driver which was hard to be. Because you didn't have access to a car for practice, and it was illegal to practice without a driving instructor. And each time you fail the test, you would have to start over and pay about the same amount of money to retake it. That was how the driving school made its money, and the corruption was so obvious that bribing felt normal.

But the day you get your driver's license, you were as happy as someone who just graduated from college. Because a driver license came with a lot of job opportunities, especially for those who didn't have a high school diploma or a college degree. You could get a job as a taxi driver or a bus driver, and if you were lucky enough you could even get a job in the government as a chauffeur. Which in that case would make it a dream job because you would get the benefits of a government pension, health insurance and a guaranteed retirement package. So, a driver's license made a lot of people's dreams come true and helped them take care of their family.

Chapter 4

At last, my father was ready and two hours later, after we had breakfast, I was sitting in the passenger seat, and we were driving to the airport. My mother stayed home to get the party ready for my graduation and the preparations to welcome Sharon. The weather was nice with few cars on the road, but still my father was driving slowly as usual under the speed limit. My father never believed in driving fast to be on time but believed in leaving early for any appointment to save time and avoid any accidents.

"One should always pace himself to avoid any stressful situation". He'd say.

For my father, everything in life was about saving. It was maybe the math teacher in him. Saving time, saving money, and saving children by helping them get an education. Those were the qualities of wisdom that he had. But I was worrying about us being late and Sharon having to wait for us in a place she had never been to, and there for a first impression.

But once again, my father was right. Slowly and surely, we arrived at the airport twenty minutes early, and as we waited outside, we heard a voice on the intercom speakers.

"The plane arriving from New York, JFK International airport will be thirty minutes late".

After arriving twenty minutes early, we now had to wait close to an hour. And waiting for Sharon's plane to arrive was more painful than my father's driving. I couldn't stand still, so I walked back and forth on the sidewalk to pass time while my father sat in the car to read the newspaper.

Fifty minutes later her plane landed. My father and I stood not too far from the exit door holding a sign in my hand reading.

"Welcome to Africa Sharon".

And as we watched each passenger go by, I was looking for anything, a sign that could help me identify her, a woman in her twenties, tall and beautiful with an American look. So, we waited until every passenger came out of the plane, but still there was no sign of Sharon anywhere. I didn't know where to look anymore nor what to think about what had just happened. So, I pulled her letter out of my pocket to check the date and time again hoping I was wrong, only to see it was the correct date and time. I was disappointed, and with my head looking down at the ground for an answer, I felt my father's arm around my shoulders.

"Let's wait a little more, maybe she is still in the back at Customs". My father said.

I wanted to believe him, but I thought my father was just trying to make me feel better. However, it made more sense that she was late because she was still in customs. Ten minutes went by and still no sign of her. After the taxis cleared the passengers pick up area, my father asked me to look across the street, and right in front of my eyes was the most beautiful woman standing there by herself with her luggage. At first look, I wasn't quite sure if it was really Sharon, because to my surprise she looked different from the picture I had of her in my mind. And from the look on her face, she might have been thinking the same thing about me too.

As we kept on looking at each other from a distance, across the street for a few seconds, I showed her the sign with her name on. She smiled and nodded her head to confirm. I smiled back and walked toward her, but I remained a bit skeptical.

She was about 5".8 tall with dark hair, and her beautiful slim face made her oval eyes look bigger. She was wearing a pair of blue jeans with a short sleeve white linen shirt, and looking at her standing there, she looked like a model on a magazine cover.

"Sharon?" I asked.

"Yes". She replied, and asked a bit hesitant in her American accent,

"Dieudonné?"

"Yes, nice to finally meet you and welcome to Africa".

I shook her hand and we kissed on both cheeks before introducing her to my father.

"It's nice to meet you Sharon, welcome to Africa". My father said.

"Me too, thank you".

I put her luggage in the trunk and opened the door for her as we sat in the back of the car next to each other like old friends. But contrary to old friends, we were strangely not talking for about a minute. One of us was waiting for the other to start the conversation with the obvious first question. My father was quietly driving home under the same speed limit pretending not to notice anything about our silence in the back. Only this time I enjoyed the slow drive home better with Sharon by my side, and wishing it never ended.

Although we were both happy to finally meet, it was quite apparent that our silence was due to the unexpected discovery of ourselves. And no matter how hard we tried to hide our discomfort, the look on our faces still left us wondering who would ask the question. Because the one thing we avoided talking about through our correspondence was now the main obstacle in front of us.

Here I was sitting next to her, 6".1 tall with blonde hair and blue eyes. My white skin had now been tanned by the hot sun through the years of living in Africa. I looked more reddish than white, but I liked it, because it made me feel more African. So, I was proud to say to anyone that Cote d'Ivoire was my country.

I dreamed of Sharon to be everything but a different race. So, I was quite taken by surprise to see that she was black, and neither could she believe her own eyes when she first saw me. The look on her face at the airport said pretty much everything. She never would have imagined in her wildest dreams that the person waiting for her at the airport in West Africa, would have been a white man. And that might have been the reason why I didn't see her as she came out of the airport, not paying any attention to me or my sign, because she was expecting to see anyone but a white man.

After more than a year of writing to each other we came to believe through our letters that we must have been alike. And because we had more in common than most people would have hoped for, each one of us believed in their heart that the other was like them, of the same race. And after all, being both graduate students and open-minded people, we thought no matter what one looked like, it wouldn't affect us.

But here we were faced with the reality of life, the pigmentation of our skin color was now the barrier in front of us that we needed to cross as we kept silent. In my case, although her race was unexpected, it didn't matter to me, because I've always considered myself an African. So, I was as happy as one could have been to have her by my side, but I was more concerned how she felt about me being white.

"How was your flight?" I asked.

"I thought you would never ask". She said smiling. "It was nice". And after a quick pause she asked.

"Why didn't you ever mention in any of your letters that you were white?"

"I thought race didn't matter to you, since you asked at the beginning of the correspondence not to exchange any photos". I replied quietly.

"Yes, race didn't matter, but a white man from West Africa is not so common, wouldn't you agree?" She asked and before I could answer her question, she continued.

"I would not have asked you if you were white, if you told me that you were from Eastern Europe, because that would be mostly expected".

"I agree, but you never said anything about you being black either, as you well know there are blacks, whites and other races living in the United States also". I replied with a smile.

"But could you at least have told me that you had blue eyes?" she said jokingly.

And to our surprise we heard my father laughing. And I looked in his rear-view mirror from my seat to see his eyes looking at us, which also made us laugh. He had been listening to our conversation all this time. I guess it was to be expected, because after all the car wasn't big enough for a private conversation. Then I remembered what my father said to me at the airport after meeting Sharon.

"I am looking forward to your conversation with Sharon driving home". He said jokingly as he was surprised as I was of her race.

But at last, a laugh was all we needed to quickly overcome the race barrier and be comfortable with one another to start a long and friendly conversation home, until my father parked his car in the garage as we arrived. My father walked Sharon inside the house while I carried the luggage to her bedroom. Then I introduced Sharon to my mother, and as she leaned over to shake her hand, my mother gently pulled her into her arms to give her a big hug.

"Akwaba, welcome to Africa". My mother said with a big smile.

"Thank you for having me in your house".

We could hear the music playing outside in the backyard from the living room, and as we walked outside, to Sharon's surprise, there was a tent for a party with about fifty people waiting for us. I then told her it was a party for my graduation which was planned for last week, but my parents and I decided to wait for her arrival so we could all celebrate together and use the occasion to welcome her in our home.

"Thank you, and congratulations."

"You're welcome, it's our pleasure to have you".

There were two long tables on each side of the tent, and the center was for the dance floor. The first table had all kinds of African food, from my favorite peanut butter sauce to okra sauce, eggplant sauce, fried plantains, and yams. My mother also made some French fries with fried chicken in case Sharon didn't like the African food. The second table had different types of fresh fruit straight from the farm, bananas, pineapples, oranges, and mangoes. The fruits were nicely ripe each with its own sweet smell. Everything on the tables looked delicious and beautiful, it was like a buffet in a four-star restaurant.

After I introduced Sharon to everyone, I walked her through the whole menu and described to her each food and what it was made of. Then I made two plates of peanut butter sauce with chicken and white rice for both of us. As we sat at the table to eat with the music playing in the background, I could see everybody patiently waiting for Sharon to take her first bite to see her reaction. But all we heard after her first bite was a sound.

"Humm!"

It was the sound of someone with a good appetite for a good meal. A sound that I found myself making many times while eating my mother's food. Her positive attitude and open mind to try her first African food brought a smile to everybody's face.

"In America, we eat peanut butter with jelly on a piece of bread. Never thought one could make a sauce out of it that would taste this good". She said.

Each one of us sitting around the table wanted to know more about her country, America. What was life like? How tall were the buildings, and was everybody as tall as we've seen on TV in the NBA? We were asking her all these questions, and every answer she gave us made us more curious about her country. She answered all our questions with details, and we listened to her with attention and envy. We even followed the motion of her hands when she was describing things, it was almost like watching a movie where she was the star.

It was just beautiful to listen to the sound of her voice, speaking from time to time the little French she knew with her American accent talking about her country as I helped her along the way with the translation. The United States of America, a country that was so far away, but seemed so close to us through pictures in magazines and movies on TV.

As the day went on, we talked, ate more, and danced. I then asked her to step outside for some fresh air. As we sat outside on the front porch, she opened her purse and handed me a small box.

"This is your graduation present. You didn't think I would forget to bring a gift?" she said smiling.

It was a small square box nicely wrapped with a shiny red paper. I couldn't believe she thought to buy me a gift for my graduation. A congratulation was good enough for me. So, it didn't matter what was in the box because the gesture alone showed what a kind and thoughtful person she was. I unwrapped the box gently and opened it with excitement. To my surprise it was a beautiful Casio watch, which I put on my wrist right away. The watch was black with a rubber band and had four push buttons, it looked like it could survive any terrain and was specially made for Africa.

"Thank you! I wasn't expecting such a nice gift".
"Do you like it?" She asked a bit unsure.

"Like it, no I love it". I replied with the biggest smile.

As I was admiring my new watch on my wrist, she said quietly.
"You know, it was a good idea that we never exchanged any photos".

"Why?" I asked, surprised.
"Because I don't think I would have given myself a chance to know you, if I knew from the beginning that you were white".

"Why?" I asked again, a bit confused, thinking that race was never an issue.

"You see, I have a lot of white friends, so I never viewed myself as a racist person. But because of racism in society toward black people, I never saw myself dating a white man nor being married to one". She replied sadly with a soft voice.

I looked her in the eyes and said.

"That makes it two of us".

"Really, you feel the same way?" she asked surprised and a bit relieved.

"Yes, but in a different way".

"How different?" She asked, confused.

So, I decided to elaborate a lot more on my answer.

"As you can see, I'm a white man who has spent his entire life in Africa. But each time I went to France on vacation to visit my grandparents, and I saw the way African people were sometimes "viewed by some white people, it made me feel like a foreigner among the people of my own race. But still I wasn't mad, because I've always believed in my heart that prejudice and racism are two things that remind us of who we are as human beings. That no matter what college degrees we had or what race we are, we remain imperfect. And to know that in Africa I wasn't treated any differently among my African friends. It made me proud to call Cote d'Ivoire my home. Because the African people welcomed me and my parents with open arms and showed us love and kindness.

"And as I learned from my own experience, that in life if we don't take the time to know the people next to us solely based on their character, no matter their race, we would always be judgmental of them to make us feel better about ourselves. Our own prejudice would blind us not to try to know them simply because they look different from us. But it's usually a complex that we have about our own self-esteem and the fear of the unknown that's stopping us from befriending them.

"But as always as anything else in life, when we give ourselves a chance to truly try to know the people around us for who they are, we stop seeing them in our eyes through the color of their skin and start to see them as we see ourselves, like any human being with good intentions. Then we realize that we have more in common than we first thought. Because it's sad to say, but we are all equal in poverty regardless of our race".

After listening attentively, she asked.

"How did you come to that conclusion?"

"What do you mean?"

"That everyone has good intentions". She replied.

"Because I believe deep down within each of us no matter our race, we're all looking for the same thing, somebody to talk to, someone to love and be loved or just to be accepted. We are looking for a true friend to love us for who we are, so we all have very much the same intention". I replied.

"You're right, I never thought of it like that". Then she asked.

"Are you always this optimistic about race?"

"Yes, I am, living in Africa and having friends of different races with different backgrounds loving each other like brothers and sisters, taught me there is more to our skin color that unifies us than separates us. Look at me, I'm white, and I know because I can see it now, but when I was born, I didn't know what race I would be nor did you. Sadly, society and education tried to make us believe that we were different from each other, and that one was perhaps even better than the other by the color of his skin. But I believe our skin color was for God to show us the beauty of mankind. In a sense it would have been boring if we were all one race in the entire world". I replied with a big smile, and she nodded her head in agreement, it was a good feeling.

"So, what do you think about interracial marriages and their children growing up in today's society?" She asked a bit pessimistically as if she wanted to challenge me even more.

"Why?"

"Because that was the main reason why I decided not to date outside my race. I didn't want my children to grow up in a society where they will be judged every day of their lives based on their skin color".

I felt like that question was personally directed to me, because if we were to be together one day, our children would be biracial. So, if there was to be a chance for love between Sharon and me, it was the only time I had to give her my best convincing argument. I paused for a few seconds to gather my thoughts.

"I've always been optimistic about the future, otherwise life would not be worth living if one doesn't believe that tomorrow will be a better day".

"Even if you don't know what tomorrow will bring?" She asked.

"Yes, I still do because an unpredictable tomorrow is what makes life exciting. It gives us hope, something to look forward to, a second chance to a new day to correct the mistakes of yesterday. So, a new opportunity to pick ourselves up and try harder the second time around to make it a better day. For that I believe that the biracial children of tomorrow, no matter where they come from will grow up in a better society. Because there will be too many of them from different races to realize that our skin color is just a pigmentation of who we are on the surface, but we are all the same human being on the inside".

She sat there quietly without saying a word, so to break her silence I said.

"You know I dreamed about this exact moment".

"What moment?" She asked, surprised.

"You and I sitting here side by side talking about everything about life and enjoying ourselves, just being happy to have met. And guess what?"

"What?"

"My dream just came true".

And out of nowhere she asked.

"Did you kiss me in your dream too?"

Her question caught me by surprise, and I was a little bit hesitant to answer. But I said.

"Yes".

"You know sometimes, dreams do come true if you believe in them". She said.

As I was listening to her, something in me wanted to kiss her or ask if I could kiss her, but I was too afraid to try because the same thing was also holding me back for fear of rejection. So, I sat there happy with her last sentence about dreams coming true if you believe in them. It gave me hope for love and a future romantic friendship. So, in my own head I was also dreaming of love with Sharon and I being together one day.

It gave me hope for love and a future romantic friendship.

We had been outside more than forty-five minutes, so we decided to go back inside the house where everybody was waiting to say good-bye to Sharon before leaving for the night. After everyone left, it was time to go to bed. I walked her to her bedroom and showed her where everything was.

Chapter 5

The next morning Sharon woke up around ten o'clock, still tired from her trip. I invited her for coffee at the main shopping center, so that she could also call her parents from a pay phone to let them know she arrived in Africa safely. After she spoke to her parents, I ordered two cups of coffee and found us a table outside on the terrace. Everybody was looking at her from a distance with admiration. Although I didn't know how she felt about me yet, I was just happy to be sitting across the table from her and calling her my friend. And after the nice conversation we had the night before, her beauty wasn't just in my eyes it was also in my heart, for I was slowly falling in love with her. She took her first sip of coffee and politely asked.

"How did your parents end up living in Africa and for you to call Cote d'Ivoire your home with so much passion?"

"I've been waiting for you to ask me that question to tell you, my story. You see, my parents first came to Africa on vacation one summer twenty-five years ago and fell in love with the kindness of the people and the warm weather. After a wonderful summer vacation, they went back to France with nothing more than the memories of Cote d'Ivoire and its beautiful coastal beaches.

"But a month later after their arrival, my mother found out that she was pregnant with me. It was the most joyful day of my parent's lives, because after trying for many years to have a child in vain, and the doctor having told my mother she could not have a child. And at last, when they were no longer expecting anything, my mother got pregnant nowhere else than in Africa. So, in my parent's eyes I was a miracle baby, that was the reason after I was born, they named me, Dieudonné, which means, in French, a gift from God or given by God.

"Now happier than ever as a complete family, they went back to their daily lives looking forward to the future and watching me grow. But as the months went by each day, they spent with me reminded them of Africa. Then one day they concluded that maybe my birth was a sign that they should go back to Africa and offer their teaching services as gratitude to the country that gave them the chance to have a child. They quit their teaching jobs a few months later, packed their staff and moved to Cote d'Ivoire. They stayed here ever since to start a new chapter of their lives, became part of the community, and called Cote d'Ivoire their lucky home".

By the time I was done telling her my story, she had tears streaming down her beautiful face.

"Why are you crying?"

"I'm sorry, but I couldn't hold back my tears at such a beautiful story of gratefulness and unselfishness from your parents. I wonder if I could have done the same thing".

"Yes, you could have, you would be surprised how sometimes the circumstances in life make us take the unexpected decision for reasons that we can't explain, and so making the hardest decision seems easy". I said. "And now it's your turn to tell me something I don't know about you".

I was hoping to hear a story about her love life to give me a starting point to talk about my own feelings.

"I was born and raised in New York, my mother is a professor at New York University and my father a United States senator". She said with a quiet voice toward the end of her sentence as if she didn't want anyone else to hear it.

Surprised, I sat there in silence with my coffee mug in my hand, and my mouth still opened, but I was unable to take a sip or say a word. I slowly put my coffee back on the table thinking maybe she was joking about her father being a United States senator. Then she nodded her head up and down to confirm what she said. That was when I realized she was telling me the truth.

"Why didn't you ever tell me that your father was a United States senator?"

And right there she could see the fear in my eyes. She reached across the coffee table to hold my hand trying to reassure me that everything was okay.

"You don't have to be afraid about my father being a US senator, trust me he is a wonderful man. And the reason why I never told you first was for security reasons, and second, I wasn't sure how you would have reacted if you knew who my father was".

Strangely we never talked about our parents in any of our letters, so it never crossed my mind that the person I was corresponding with, that their father could have been a United States senator. I was thinking to myself that might have been the primary reason why she didn't want to exchange any photo through our correspondence.

"You were right not to say anything about your father. Because if I had known that he was a United States senator, I would have been hesitant to write to you or say some of the things I said in my letters".

"That was the reason I never said anything, because I wanted you to know me for who I am and not as the daughter of a Senator, so that you could freely write and be yourself".

"But now I'm afraid that if you were to be sick, even a simple headache may get me in trouble with the Secret Service". I said jokingly.

"You would not get in trouble for something that small, it has to be a little more than a headache". She replied laughing, and I couldn't help but laugh with her.

I've always believed that a good relationship between two people starts by telling the truth about each other's lives and what they like and dislike. By doing so, they may learn what they have in common to be the best of friends. Because from the words they say would come the answer for someone who's looking for friendship or true love.

But here I was now with a dilemma, scared of the truth and afraid of the future, because the daughter of a United States senator was never on my love wish list. I couldn't see how she could fall in love with me, especially being from Africa. So, the hope I had for a romantic relationship was fast disappearing.

"I would like to ask you a couple favors". She said unexpectedly.
"I will do anything for you".

I replied eagerly without even knowing what the favors were.

"First favor, promise me, you won't tell your parents or anyone else about my father being a senator".

"Why?" I asked surprised.

"Because I wouldn't want to receive any special treatment that could affect the accuracy of my research about African culture. And after seeing your reaction, I'm afraid most people will feel the same as you did, a little scared".

It wasn't an easy promise to keep, because of the close relationship I had with my parents. But I agreed to keep it secret knowing how important her thesis was.

"And what is the second favor?" I asked anxiously.

She took another sip of her coffee which got me a little bit worried and wondering if I didn't promise too much too soon. Then she asked.

"Would you be able to take me to a village where we could stay for the next four weeks for my research?"

Although I was confused by her second request, I was still relieved compared to her first one.

"Why the village?"

"Coming to Africa and thinking that you were African, my plan was to stay with you in your village so that I could participate in the daily lives of the village people and have you as an interpreter".

She went ahead and explained to me in detail her plan and goal for the next four weeks in Africa. Where she wanted to go, and what she wanted to do to get as much information as possible to write her thesis. As I was listening to her, I was also planning in my head a trip to the village. Although I wasn't the African man she was expecting, I was also not the typical white man from Africa either. Because I knew where to take her, and the one thing she didn't know about me was that I spent some of my holidays during the school year with my Godfather in the village, and I also could speak the dialect. So, I proceeded to tell her about him.

"I have a Godfather who lives in the village, his name is Konan. But I call him Uncle Konan. My father and Uncle Konan have been friends for more than twenty years. They met at the same high school where they were both teaching. A few years ago, after Uncle Konan's father, who was the village chief, passed away, he was obligated to take an early retirement to succeed his father as the new village chief. He is a very kind and humble man with a brain full of knowledge about African traditions and culture. I think you will learn a lot from him".

She was surprised and happy to know that she would be able to go to the village, and she was also excited to meet Uncle Konan, the village chief.

"I don't have enough time, so could we leave today?" "I think you should get another day of rest before the trip to the village". I replied.

And as I could see the excitement in her eyes, so was her love for Africa. She didn't just want to write a story about the culture, but she also wanted to be part of the experience and for that she was willing to live in a village and learn directly from the people. So, for her to have traveled from America to Africa to meet me and learn about the culture, I was willing to help her any way possible with her research.

"What was your parent's reaction about coming to Africa and living in a village?"

"My parents were worried at first, because Africa in the eyes of most Americans through the news we see on TV is a dangerous place with unstable political parties. So, to reassure them about my safety, I gave them all the information needed about you and your country in case something was to go wrong. And eventually they agreed that there was not a better place to experience the culture, than be among the people. But also visiting Africa has always been a dream of mine. That was why I picked for my thesis topic, Life and Culture in Africa".

"I share your parents' concern, and I can assure you that you will be safe during your entire stay. And I promise you will have the best time of your life in Africa, memories for you to remember when you go back to America".

I was impressed by her parents' understanding to let her go. Although they were concerned for her safety, they were still willing to let her follow her dream even if it meant going into the jungle of Africa to write her thesis. It was only her second day in Africa, and once again I was learning something about life from her. She made me believe that everyone can have a dream. And a dream wasn't just something that we had in mind. But a dream is the thing that guides our determination through the difficulties, and obstacles of life to achieve our goal. Because a dream gives us hope and makes us believe that anything is possible in life if we put our heart to it.

After we got home from the coffee shop later that morning, I told my parents the news of Sharon writing her thesis about African culture, and why she needed to live in the village for her research. Although my parents wanted her to stay for a few more days, they understood as teachers themselves that time was of the essence for her research. So, my father volunteered to give us a ride to the village the following day and use the occasion to visit his best friend Konan, the village chief.

Chapter 6

I have always looked forward to each trip to the village, but this one was the most special. It was a dream trip, because it could not have been a better opportunity for me to spend time with Sharon and impress her with my knowledge of village life. It was an experience I wanted to share with her, hoping it will bring us closer together.

My father spoke to Uncle Konan on his mobile phone about our arrival the night before. And the next day after we had lunch, Sharon and I once again were sitting in the backseat of my father's car on the road to the village as we did two days earlier at the airport, only this time we could not stop talking.

"How should I behave with the village people?" She asked.

"Be respectful and don't say no to anything they offer you, because it will be viewed as a sign of disrespect. If you only do that, you will be okay, as they will show you their kindness in return". I replied.

We arrived at the village an hour later. The village was called Konankro, it was a small and beautiful village named after the great grandfather of Uncle Konan, now the village chief. There was one main road that crossed the village to the next town, and next to the road was a big tree where the children were playing. The tree was also used by taxi and minibus drivers as a stop area to drop off and pick up new passengers. And under the tree there was a young girl selling some cookies in a basket, not too far from her was a man sitting in a chair at a small table selling some cigarettes.

It was about three o'clock in the afternoon. The farmers were coming back home from their long and hard-working day at the farm. The farmer and his family were all walking in line with their children one after another. The oldest son was first in line as the designated watcher to clear the road for any trouble coming from the front, and behind him was his mother with her baby daughter gently strapped on her back. The rest of the siblings were following their mother, and in the back of the line was their father walking as the guardian, the protector of his family from any surprise coming from behind.

To a city man, the life of a farmer was just life on the farm. But to the farmer, farming was everything he had and loved. It was the fruit of his labor for the well-being of his family and their everyday lives. Although farming was hard work and demanded a lot of patience, the farmer always knew that there was no such thing as a silly job. Because he knew even if a job didn't make you rich, it guaranteed you of your dignity.

As I stood next to the car to say hello to the farmers passing by, and watched the families walk into the village, I could read on the farmer's face all the hard work he had gone through his entire life to take care of his family and trying to make a better future for his children. The sweat coming down between each wrinkle on the farmer's strong and tired face was a sign of endurance and determination to preserve his dignity as a man through his hard work. His bent back and folded shoulders on his old body frame showed the heavy load he carried through his work. But still, his strong and rough hands were those of a caring husband and loving father.

My father's car was surrounded by a group of young kids happy to help us carry our luggage. And as we walked inside the chief's house, Uncle Konan shook my hand and I felt it in my entire body. Here he was retired and the village chief, now a farmer himself. We hugged each other like father and son, that was how special he was to me. He hugged my father, his best friend, for a little longer to show the affection between old friends. Then gently shook Sharon's hand with a bright smile to welcome her.

As we sat in the living room, Uncle Konan asked his children to bring us some water to drink, before asking my father the reason for our visit. My father then introduced Sharon to Uncle Konan and his wife, and gave them the details of our visit. He asked Uncle Konan if he could help Sharon with her research about African culture during her stay for the next four weeks in the village.

"This is wonderful, it will be an honor to have her in our village". Uncle Konan said and continued. "I will teach her our traditions and culture, and I will introduce her to everyone in the village, so that she can get all the help she needs".

Then he introduced Sharon to his children and told them to make sure she felt welcome and had what she needed during her stay.

"Thank you very kindly". Sharon said to Uncle Konan and his family.

Uncle Konan was simply amazed to see an American with such an interest in African culture, and for that reason alone he was willing to do anything in his power to accommodate Sharon. I could see the joy in his smile and the excitement on his face knowing he wanted to talk to Sharon about Africa. And Sharon could only sit there with admiration for such kindness from the village chief, a man she just met and who wanted to tell her the story of his people and his village.

The village chief was not democratically elected, but he inherited the position from his father, and his father also inherited from his father before him, and so on. The chief was the most powerful man in the village. He was the village chief and the supreme judge, no matter his age he was to be respected. The chief was to be humble and wise, and was always to remain impartial to any dispute among the villagers. For that, the chief worked closely with a group of elders as his personal advisers to help him in his decision making, because his word was final as a supreme judge.

For a small conflict between two parties, the village chief may ask the party that was at fault for a simple apology to the other. But in a case of a serious dispute between two families, he may ask one family to compensate the other based on emotional pain that the other family suffered. And the compensation could vary from a bottle of whisky to a live chicken and sometimes even a goat to be given to the family. The compensation was to be reasonable and appropriate not to embarrass either family. All of this is done in good faith to reconcile the families, to bring peace and harmony among the people to keep the village together.

But one of the most important roles of the chief was to be the guardian of the values, customs, and tradition of the village for his people. By doing so, he applies the rules they must all live by including himself according to the traditions.

Later that afternoon, after we had dinner together, my father said goodbye and was back on the road to the city. And Uncle Konan, as the village chief, invited the villagers to a general meeting to introduce Sharon. He requested that everyone help her to the best of their ability in her research, with me playing the role of the interpreter. We spent the rest of the time talking to the village people and Sharon making plans in her notebook with each person for her first week's schedule.

The next morning, a new day started for Sharon and me. She woke up early, brushed her teeth and washed her face like the rest of the family. And to the surprise of everyone she asked Uncle Konan if she could come to the farm with them for her first experience. And without hesitation Uncle Konan said.

"Yes".

He thought the farm was the best place to start her research, and with her backpack on her shoulders, and both of us wearing shorts and tee-shirts, the farm became our first destination. It was about six o'clock in the morning and the sun was slowly coming out. The humidity was everywhere in the air, and we could feel the sweat on our skin as we walked into the forest. Our shoes and legs were getting wet from the drops of water left on the weeds by the early morning fog.

The deeper we went into the forest, the quieter it got, and so, we could hear loud and clear the birds singing. The sound of the crickets mixed with the bird's songs created a musical cacophony, which echoed back to our ears and gave us the impression of being followed.

Although it wasn't my first trip to the farm, it reminded me of my first time walking on this path with Uncle Konan, so I could guess what Sharon might have been thinking. Because as usual in the forest, after walking for a period of time, everything started to look the same. The only color we could see all around us, was green from the weeds on the ground to the big trees with their leaves that stopped our view from the distance. And with nothing more to see on the horizon, the road to the farm seemed endless as our pathway was slowly closing on itself behind us.

"Are we there yet?"

"Almost". I replied.

And after the third time she stopped asking, instead she gave me a look from time to time. I knew she was getting tired of walking, especially with the humidity, and when I finally told her we had arrived, she didn't believe me. So, I pointed to her between the trees a small pavilion with the roof made of palm tree leaves, and next to it was a cabin made of mud and clay. The cabin was used for sleeping by the family in case the weather was too bad to return to the village. Then I asked her to look at the time on her watch. She nodded her head and smiled.

"It's only been forty minutes, but it felt like we were walking forever".

No one was happier than Sharon when we arrived at the farm. She looked around the farm, touched the mango tree and looked up in the sky as if she was looking for something missing, then she said.

"It's beautiful. I'm happy to be here".

I guess she was just admiring nature. We all sat down under the pavilion to get ourselves organized before Uncle Konan gave us a tour of the farm. It was a big and beautiful farm with five acres of coffee and cocoa. There was also plantains, yams, and different kinds of vegetables for the family consumption. Sharon began her day by asking questions about everything from the plants to the soil in which the farmer grew his food. She was as excited to see all the beautiful ripe fruit on the trees, as she was curious about the cocoa trees. And for her love of chocolate, she seemed more fascinated with the cocoa fruit and wanted to know everything about it. With a notebook and a pen in her hand, I was ready to start the interpretation when she asked Uncle Konan her first question.

"How is chocolate made from this fruit? And how do you grow cocoa?"

Uncle Konan smiled before holding in the palm of his left hand a cocoa fruit, and with a machete in his right hand he cracked it wide open without hurting himself. The cocoa beans inside the shell were covered with white fibers attached to each other. He then asked Sharon to take one bean out to eat as he did himself. And he asked her not to swallow the bean, but only to eat the white fiber around it.

"It's not as sweet as I thought it would be, and it doesn't taste anything like chocolate". She said surprised.

With only the bean left in her mouth, he asked her to take it out as he was already holding his in the hand. And like a science teacher, he carefully cut the bean in two pieces with a knife to show her the dark brown color inside.

"This is what chocolate is made of". He said.

Then Uncle Konan grabbed a couple chairs and asked us to sit down. And I knew right there it was going to be a long and teachable moment for Sharon.

"I will start by answering your second question first. How do we grow cocoa? He said rhetorically. You need patience and time for a cocoa plant to grow into a tree, and start producing its fruit. For that, the farmer must take care of the cocoa plant every day as if he was taking care of a baby. Because it is a very delicate plant that demands a lot of attention.

"Before the farmer could start planting the cocoa plants, he must first get the soil ready by cutting all the weeds on the ground and burning it. This part of the process is not only to fertilize the soil, but most important of all is to stop the weeds from tangling with the cocoa plants and stop its growth. Next, the farmer must plant a plantain plant for each future cocoa plant. Because the cocoa plant being very sensitive to the sun will die within days when exposed to the sunlight, and the farmer would have lost all his investment and hard work.

"To avoid that, the farmer must wait approximately nine months for the banana plant to fully grow. And finally, it will be time to start planting the cocoa plant next to each banana tree.

The cocoa plant will then grow in the shade of the banana tree leaves protected from the sun. As time goes and the cocoa plant grows into a tree, it will be able to protect itself from the sun on its own. The farmer will then cut down most of the banana trees to make room for the cocoa tree to fully grow. It will take at least four years for the cocoa plant to grow to a tree and start producing its first fruit.

"And while the farmer waits for the next four years for his first harvest of cocoa, the plantain will be the source of income and food for his family livelihood. He will use a portion of plantain to feed his family and the rest will be for sale for the family basic needs. At last, after four years of waiting and hard work, comes the harvest season, the farmer and his family will extract the beans from each cocoa fruit and put it in bags to be fermented for a couple days. At the end of the fermentation process, the cocoa beans will be put on a mat to dry under the sun for a few days. The farmers would then put the dried cocoa beans in bags to be sold to a cocoa dealer, which will be later shipped overseas to be transformed into chocolate."

Uncle Konan concluded the story of cocoa with a smile of a man that was proud of his work, and in some ways felt like he had his hands on each chocolate bar.

"Wow! What a long process". she said, mesmerized.
"I can't believe it takes that many years for a cocoa tree to start producing its first fruit, and how much work needs to be done".

That was the reason he said.
"It was like taking care of a baby".

"How many seasons do you have? And how did you know when to start planting?"

"We only have two seasons, the dry season, and the rainy season. Water and the weather being the two main factors for a successful harvest. it is upon the farmer to study the weather to know when it will rain to start planting and how close was the dry season to start the harvest before it was too late".

Then Uncle Konan pointed his finger in the direction of a tree and said.
"You see that big tree over there with all its leaves? During the dry season it will be left standing without any leaves on".

Curious still, she asked.

"How bad can the dry season be to a farmer and its crops?"

"It depends. If the dry season lasts longer than usual it could be devastating for a farmer. But the dry season is not always the bearer of bad news, because it has its benefits. It gives the soil time to heal and the farmer time to rest after a long harvest".

"How does the farmer know so much about the weather and the plants?"

"I learned it from my parents, and they too learned it from their parents and so on".

As I was interpreting her questions and Uncle Konan answers back and forth, Sharon was writing in her notebook page after page, listening to every word of Uncle Konan.

"I have one more question".

"Sure, I'm here to answer all of your questions".

"Why do you come to the farm so early in the morning when you have all day, and you are your own boss?"

"Very good question". He said with a smile. "It's because the weather is unpredictable and knowing that every decision I make depends on the weather, it is important for the farmer to come early in the morning to do as much work as possible in case there is a change in the weather".

"That makes a lot of sense to me now". She said.

After the nice and long educational conversation about cocoa. We spent the rest of the day helping with some farm work, and from time to time we enjoyed some fresh fruit straight from the trees. We all took a break at twelve o'clock and had some grilled plantain with smoked fish for lunch. And a couple hours later, we helped clean up the farm and it was time to go back to the village.

By the time we got home in the afternoon, after a long day of work at the farm, we could feel the pain of the distance in our legs. We were both tired and ready for some rest.

"This was one of the best experiences of my life. And after spending a day on the farm, I understand now how hard the farmer must work to take care of his family, but also how much knowledge he has of nature and his environment".

"This was just the beginning, there will be even better days full of new life experiences to come". I said.

From that day on, life in the village with Sharon went on as planned, each day was a new adventure and a new life experience. She met with every person in the village needed for her research, while still finding time to go to the farm occasionally.

One morning as Sharon and I were standing outside, we saw a group of women with their daughters coming back from the well. Each woman was carrying a big bucket of water on top of her head, with her little girl walking by her side also carrying her own small bucket of water. The women rolled a piece of cloth in a circle like cushion to put between the bucket and their heads to carry the water weight and ease the pain on their heads. Surprised and curious, Sharon asked Uncle Konan's wife.

"What is the water for?"

"The water is for daily use". Mrs. Konan replied and decided to elaborate a lot more for Sharon.

"The women make the same trip twice a day. One in the morning and the other later in the afternoon. And for each trip they take the same quantity of water needed per family, because water is scarce and must be used wisely not to dry out the well. The morning water is used for the family's daily needs, cooking and drinking, and the afternoon water is for showering".

"Why do the women in the village always work together?" She asked.

"We work together because it makes work fun, and the time goes by faster".

As I interpreted Sharon word per word, Mrs. Konan concluded with the voice of a caring mother.

"But we also believe that if we help one another, God will bless us and our family. That is why with the limited resources that we have in the village, we look after each other and each other's children as our own".

Over the coming days, she invited Sharon with me along to all the women's meetings and activities to help her understand the culture, and the importance of a woman's role in the family and the community. Sharon appreciated every moment and gained a lot of respect for the women's contribution in the village. She also learned that the women were an essential part of the household that held the family together. Because the women understood that even if the men were the hardest working people in the farm, the woman's role was indispensable in raising the children and caring for her husband.

Chapter 7

It was Friday morning, soon to be Saturday and already our second week together. Saturday was a slow workday for the farmer and Sunday was a day off for him and his family. But still the farmer would go to the farm on the weekend by himself or sometimes with one of his sons to check on his traps hoping to catch some bush meat. Some bush meat would always be a welcoming surprise for his wife and children to have some meat for dinner for a few days. But Saturday was also the best day of the week for boys to meet girls at a party.

The weeks seemed to come faster than expected. In fear of not telling Sharon my true feelings before it was too late, I decided to make the coming Saturday a special day for us. I wanted to tell her everything once for all. I was tired of hiding my feelings because I was too afraid of rejection from her without giving myself a chance to tell her how I truly felt about her. Standing next to her, and not knowing what to say nor where to start, I decided to get right to the point.

"Would you like to go out on a picnic tomorrow?" I asked. I was hoping it was the right way to ask an American girl out on a date.

She looked at me as if she could read my mind and replied smiling.

"Is this a date?"

"Yes". I said, a little bit hesitant and unsure of what her response would be, but only this time, I was hoping she couldn't read my mind and see how nervous I was.

"I was starting to think you would never ask". And after a short pause, she said.

"Yes of course, I would love to go out on a date with you".

What a relief it was to hear her say yes. I had already everything planned, so I was looking forward to what to bring on the date to make it romantic.

The day was finally here, it was around eleven o'clock on Saturday morning. It was a beautiful day and I vividly remember everything about that day from the brightness of the sun to the smell of the leaves. I thought about that day the night before in bed. The food I would bring to the picnic, the romantic place I would take her to, and what I would tell her to create a scene of the perfect moment for our first kiss. I played the same scene in my head over and over to the point where it felt like a dream.

I had my backpack filled with food, drinks, and a blanket. And as we walked to the picnic place, I wanted to hold her hand, but I was afraid she would feel my excitement, because my heart was beating too fast. It wasn't out of fear, each heart beat I was hearing in my chest was the sound of love, and the feeling of joy for what the future could be with her.

As we arrived at the picnic site, we could see flowers of different colors along the riverside. The smell of their sweet perfume mixed with the smell of the forest giving it a strong masculine scent of fresh wood, and with the river water running in the background made the place feel even more romantic.

I put the blanket on the ground not too far from the river, and as we sat down next to each other, I emptied my backpack. There was fruit, cheese, and a baguette of French bread with a bottle of red wine. It was a bottle of Beaujolais and two wine glasses.

"Where did you get all of this?" She asked with her eyes wide open.

"After you said yes to our date yesterday, I called my father and asked him to bring it to me through a taxi driver coming to the village, which I received this morning".

"I'm impressed, I wasn't expecting wine and cheese for lunch today. Are you trying to create a romantic French scene, Monsieur Dieudonné?"

"Yes, I figured I would try my best on our first date for a good impression. So how am I doing so far?" I asked.

"So far you're doing very well".

I opened the bottle of wine like a sommelier and gently poured some wine in both glasses.

"Let's toast to friendship and the future". I said, with my glass in my hand half full.

Then after our first drink of wine, I asked her to close her eyes for a few seconds, and when she reopened her eyes, I was holding in my hand a bright yellow flower for her.

"Do you know what flower this is?"
"It's called a sunflower in English". She replied.

"Yes, it is, in French it's called Le Tournesol which means, I have eyes only for you or you are my sunshine". I said.

She held the flower in her hand, smelled it and unexpectedly gave me a kiss on my lips before she said.

"Thank you".

And as she was pulling away, I leaned toward her to kiss her back with a long kiss of my own. It was a kiss full of love. My heartbeat became more normal to the touch of her soft lips against mine. And with my hands running through her beautiful hair, I felt like I was on top of the world. I realized then, that with all the plans I had in mind the night before, I could not have scripted the scene better myself, because as unpredictable as it was, it was the best kiss I ever had. And before we knew it, we were both passionately kissing each other as if it was the only thing that we had been waiting for our entire lives and wanted more than anything else.

We made love that day for the first time, and later laid down on the blanket next to each other holding hands with our fingers intertwined as we both quietly admired the blue sky. Right that moment, time seemed to stay still. We couldn't hear anything; it was total silence. It felt as if everything around us had stopped moving, and the sky had opened for the sun to shine its bright light only on us in our own little paradise. There was nothing to fear nor to be embarrassed by our naked bodies, for some reason although alone, we felt safe with the forest to ourselves. And all I was hoping for was the day to never end and time to never move forward, because for the first time in my life I knew what true love really felt like. So, for a few hours in the forest the world seemed perfect. I was slowly falling in love with her heartbeat by heartbeat. But strangely I wasn't the only one out of words to express their feelings, because when I turned to her and asked.

"How do you feel?"

She paused for a few seconds, and simply answered. "Never been happier". And followed up with a question of her own. "How is it possible? How is it possible? And the third time she repeated the same question word for word. "How... is... it... possible?"

"How is what possible?" I asked anxiously.
"For two people from different continents and cultures to fall in love just by communicating through writing. Please tell me Dieudonné".

Her question was a relief, because now I knew, I wasn't the only one falling in love. But the answer she was looking for, was a different story. It could have taken me hours to think of something romantic to say, or days to do some deep soul searching about the meaning of love to give her the best answer possible. But out of time and out of ideas, I decided to let my heart express itself on how we find love sometimes in the least expected place, and with the one person that we never thought of.

"You see, more often in life, love comes to us unexpectedly, and sometimes without our own knowledge. It could be just by seeing each other's face every day at work, hearing each other's voice over the phone or something as simple as reading each other's letters. But before we know, we find ourselves already in love with that person we walked past every morning without paying any attention to. Although the person might have been invisible to our eyes, but not to our heart. Because true love will always conquer any obstacles to find its other half, for love will only happen if we really believe in the power of love".

"What is the power of love?" She asked.

"It's the love that is powerful enough to go behind our own feelings without our knowledge, and bring us close to someone we never would have thought fallen in love with in life.

And after we meet that person, we realize that love was right there in front of our eyes all the time and couldn't see it".

"That was beautiful and so true. I wondered why I never thought of the power of love that way, a love that is independent of our own consent".

So, I thought that maybe it was the best time to tell her about my own experience and feelings for her and when it all started.

"I started to develop feelings for you after a couple months of writing to each other. And without having seen your picture I felt as if I knew you before. Your words in your writing were kind and caring, and made me believe in our new friendship. I imagined what a nice and beautiful woman you might be in person and couldn't wait to reply to you the next day, hoping you do the same so that I could read your response sooner to feel like I was talking to you every day. I wish I could say love at first sight, but it was for sure love through writing".

"I also felt the same way as you did from your letters. But I wasn't sure of my feelings, so I couldn't admit it to myself for fear that I was possibly falling in love with a stranger. I guess life sometimes is full of surprises and unpredictable happy moments".

And for me to add. "Yes, and that's what makes life so special and worth living. Sometimes we have a tendency of saying during a sad time that life is not worth anything. But in truth nothing is worth more than life, especially when we are in love".

She nodded her head in agreement and we kissed again. We spent the rest of the day talking about love and life, and how lucky we were to have found each other halfway around the world, and for love to bring us together in Africa. I looked at my watch, and I was surprised to see that five hours had gone by so fast.

"I didn't know it was so late, I guess for a moment time really stood still". I said.

We both laughed and started packing for the village. This time the return to the village was different, we walked back home holding hands like two high school students coming back from the prom, with an empty backpack on my shoulders, but a heart full of love and dreams. It was a wonderful feeling.

From that day on, the riverside became our favorite place to go. The connection between the water and the silence of the forest inspired her thesis writing. We also loved the romantic side of it because it always reminded us of our first date. The weeks went by as fast as they came, and each passing day was a day closer to her return to America. Until one morning, she said.

"This is my last week".

"I know. I was trying not to think about it". I replied quietly as I could hear the sadness in her voice.

Suddenly I felt alone at the thought of her leaving. After being together for three weeks and spending everyday together, I couldn't think of what my life would be without her as her departure was fast approaching. Then she said.

"I was planning on calling my parents today to tell them that I need to stay one more week to finish my research".

"This is wonderful news". I said with excitement.

I couldn't have been happier to have an extra week together, it was like getting a life extension. And this time I wanted to spend every minute with her and enjoy every second. We tried calling her parents from the village with my mobile phone, but we were unable to get any connection. So, I called my father and gave him Sharon's parents phone number and asked him to inform them of her decision to stay one more week to finish her research.

We continued our daily activities as usual, and we spent every day together as if it was our last. We went to bed late at night talking about a future that was unknown to us in a world that wasn't perfect, still we remained optimistic about what life would bring to us. And we woke up the next day to finish the conversation where we left off, it was as if we never went to sleep.

We did all this, because somewhere in our heart we were thinking of how to be together without saying so, but hoping for a miracle.

Chapter 8

The good news of an extended week didn't last too long, when three days later we came back from the farm with Uncle Konan, to find my father sitting in the living room with two other gentlemen. One was black and the other white, both well dressed in a dark blue suit with a black tie. I stood there for a few seconds confused and wondering of their presence in the village with my father. But when I turned to Sharon, to my surprise she seemed more relaxed than I was from the expression on her face. It was as if she knew who they were and why they were there.

"Is everything alright?" I asked my father.

"Don't worry, they are here for me". Sharon replied, before my father could answer.

After both gentlemen introduced themselves to us as United States secret service agents from the US embassy, they said to Sharon.

"We are here on the request of your father, the US senator, to take you back to the United States".

"Why". She asked.

"For your safety". The agent replied. "Your parents were worried about you because they learned of a terrorist attack that happened two days ago, in the neighboring country of Mali, which borders with Cote d'Ivoire. So, we are here to take you home".

Surprised by their unexpected visit to take her back to America, she asked to speak to them in private, and about ten minutes later she came back upset. I could see on her face the sadness of their answer while she was still trying to hold back her tears. She called me to her bedroom to tell me what happened.

"I told them I needed a few more days to finish my research and they said no. So, I asked them to give me at least a day to say good-bye and thank the village people for all their help and hospitality. But no matter what I said, I couldn't change their mind. Their answer remained the same because they were ordered to take me back. I'm leaving today with them for the US Embassy. I'm sorry".

Then her tears started streaming down her beautiful face, which made me realize she was really leaving and the dream of us being together one more week would never happen. I closed my eyes and I wished for a moment that it was all a bad dream. But sadly, it was as real as someone pinching me. Sitting next to her on the side of the bed, I helped wipe the tears off her face.

"Everything will be alright, and if it's meant to be, we will see each other again". I said.

And as I was helping her pack, she gently grabbed my hand and put her index finger across her mouth telling me to keep quiet. Then she got up to check that the door was tightly shut and sat close to me, and with a soft voice whispered.

"I have a plan that would allow me to stay, but I will need to ask you a couple questions first, and I would like a yes or no answer".

"Sure". I said, wondering what such a plan could be.

"Do you really love me?" She asked first.

"Yes". I replied thinking it was a trick question because the answer was so obvious. So, I thought her next question would make me doubt my first answer.

"Would you marry me tomorrow?" She asked next with a straight face.

And this time her second question took me by surprise, but I answered without any hesitation.

"Yes."

Still, I kept on thinking there must be a catch somewhere in her questioning which seemed to never come. I started to wonder if she was doubting my love for her and needed some reassurance from me to confirm her feelings before leaving for America.

"Why did you ask me those questions?

After a brief pause, she replied with a smile.

"Because I would like us to get married tomorrow".

"Is this a joke?" I asked, a little bit confused. "Because if it isn't a joke, how would we get married tomorrow knowing that you are leaving today?"

"No, it's not a joke and I really mean it". She replied. And right there, I could see in her eyes that she was sincere and meant everything she said.

"So, what is the plan?" I asked.

I was now more impatient to know the details of her plan and was willing to do anything to be together. She went ahead and explained in full detail her plan and promised to return for the wedding the next day at 3:00 pm. She told me the most important things that I needed to do in a timely manner for the wedding and insisted on one thing over and over.

"Please do not give up on waiting for me no matter how long it takes, don't lose hope. I promise to be back".

After we kissed goodbye, I came out of the bedroom still showing my disappointment like she had asked me to, in order not to bring any suspicion of the plan to anyone. My father and

Uncle Konan tried one last time to persuade the agents to change their mind in vain as they remained inflexible in their decision.

And when the village people heard the news of Sharon leaving, the women came running to the chief's house with their children by their side. They begged the agents, hoping they would be kind enough to let her stay one more day, so that they could have the opportunity to bring her a few gifts to say goodbye like it is in the African culture. But the agents didn't seem to care about their request, as they sat there quietly in their chairs until Sharon came out of the bedroom with her luggage. And as Sharon hugged everyone goodbye, no woman present had a dry face, even the children were crying.

I put her luggage in the trunk of the agent's car, and we hugged each other one last time without kissing. It was a decision we both made early to avoid any attention of our romantic relationship in front of the agents.

The children started to run after the car as the agents were driving away, waving their hands goodbye to Sharon, who was still looking at us from the rear-view window. Then something unexpected happened. Maybe out of remorse, the agents slowed down their car for the children to catch up to them and hold on to it for the next thirty seconds which felt like a few minutes. We all started to clap, because after all their refusal to let Sharon stay one more day, they showed at last to the children that they had some compassion. And as the children slowly let the car go, we watched the car make a right turn and finally disappear on the winding road.

I could see on the villager's faces as they gathered around to comfort me with their support, the sadness of Sharon's premature departure. For her to be loved by everyone in the village in such a short period of time, showed me what a wonderful person she was and how lucky I was to be soon married to her. I was now more than ever willing to do everything to make our wedding a reality. And as we walked back inside the house my father asked suddenly.

"Why didn't you tell me that her father was a United States senator?"

"I'm sorry, but I promised Sharon not to tell anyone".

"What kind of promise was that?" My father asked, a bit upset.

"I'm your father. Didn't you think that if anything was to happen to her, your mother and I would be the ones responsible for it?"

"Yes, I did, but she asked me to promise not to tell anyone, because she didn't want to receive any special treatment that could have affected the accuracy of her research. She didn't want people to be intimidated because her father was a United States senator"

In the end, both my father and Uncle Konan agreed and understood her concern, and saw how humble she was for being the daughter of a United States senator and wanted to be treated like everyone else. It was now time for me to tell my father and Uncle Konan about my conversation with Sharon.

"Sharon and I decided to get married".

Surprised, my father asked.

"When and how?"

"She just left". Uncle Konan said to emphasize my father's point.

Then both looked at each other and looked back at me in a strange way as if I was going crazy, and still were expecting an answer from me. But before I could say a word, my father said to me in a calm voice.

"I know you love her son, but she is gone".
And for Uncle Konan the wise man that he was, to add.

"Dieudonné, if you're meant to be married to each other one day, God will find a way to bring you both together".

"He did". I said.
"Who did?" Both asked stunned.

"God". I replied smiling. "But you have to listen to what I have to say first".

"Okay, we're listening". My father said.
"Sharon asked me to marry her tomorrow to which I said yes".

But before I could finish my father interrupted me again.

"We are willing to listen, but the question remains the same, how will you get married tomorrow when she is already gone and you're here by yourself?"

My father asked, a little bit concerned this time.

"But you have to let me finish talking first, so that I can explain everything to you". I replied frustrated.

"Okay! Go on". My father said, and both sat quietly. "Sharon talked about her plan to make the wedding possible. She will find a way to escape from her hotel and will be here in the village by three o'clock tomorrow afternoon. But upon her arrival she would like us to have everything ready for the wedding ceremony. She requested a city mayor to validate the marriage certificate, a priest for the religious ceremony and the village chief, so Uncle Konan for the traditional ceremony, with a camera man to videotape the whole wedding. And most important of all, she insisted not to lose hope, because no matter what happened, she promised to be here".

"But, what about the secret service agents? Will they still take her back to America after the wedding is over?" My father asked.

"No, not after we are legally married, because when she becomes my wife, they can no longer take her back against her will, so she will be able to stay here as long as she likes".

As I explained everything to my father and Uncle Konan in detail, although they remained a little bit skeptical about the whole plan, they decided nevertheless to take a chance to make the marriage possible, since Sharon was willing to risk everything to get married. My father left right away for the city to meet with his good friend the mayor, and to meet the rest of Sharon's demands.

And for Uncle Konan as the village chief, immediately ordered his drummer to call the village people to an urgent meeting at his house. As custom, the chief's drummer uses his drums as a means of communication between the chief and the village people to convey meetings, and different events in the village. The drummer interprets the chief's words through the sound of each drum beat as each beat has a specific meaning.

While standing outside by myself thinking what a day it has been and what the next twenty-four hours would be like, I could hear loud and clear the sound of the drum beat traveling in all four corners of the village. And as men and women walked toward the chief's house, I could also tell of the importance and urgency of the meeting from the villager's footsteps by how fast they were walking.

As everybody gathered in the courtyard to hear their chief speak, Uncle Konan, sitting in his big chair like a king, stood up to talk to his people.

"A few hours ago, we were all saddened to see Sharon leave without giving enough time to say good-bye to us. But I'm here to tell you today that tomorrow will be a wonderful day, it will be one of the best days in our village history to remember. Because Sharon and Dieudonné will get married, here in our village".

The chief barely finished his sentence when the villagers started applauding. And he continued.

"But to make the marriage possible I will need the help of each one of you in the village for the preparation and celebration of their wedding".

As the villagers were listening to their chief speak, although excited about the news, they looked at each other confused and intrigued with Sharon already gone. The chief then explained to them that Sharon would find a way to escape from the agents and return to the village for the wedding by three o'clock tomorrow afternoon.

"It is paramount that everybody works together as a team to get everything ready for the wedding ceremony before Sharon arrives. Because the agents will come looking for her in the village when they find out she escaped. But the good news is after Sharon and Dieudonné are married, the secret service agents can no longer take her back to America. She will be able to stay in the village as long as she would like". He concluded.

And this time, I could hear the villagers singing and shouting for joy about the wedding. From that moment, I could see the excitement on everyone's face to make the wedding possible, and what seemed like a dream a few hours ago, now felt like a reality. And if the village people were looking for revenge against the agents for having taken Sharon away, the wedding was the best source of motivation for a payback.

Right there the chief divided the villagers in four different groups each with their own assignment. He assigned to the first group of young men the responsibility of watchdog for Sharon's taxi. They would be waiting on the roadside the next day around twelve o'clock in the afternoon, about a few miles away from the entrance of the village for Sharon's taxi. And as soon as her taxi entered the village, they were advised to put an already cut tree trunk on the road as a blockade to stop the agent's car and slow their entrance into the village, until the official part of the marriage ceremony was over which shouldn't be more than fifteen minutes.

The second group of adult men were in charge of the palm tree wine, the drinks and killing the lamb. And after cleaning and cutting, the meat was to be sent to the third group, the women in charge of the cooking, and last were the women responsible for getting the traditional wedding clothes and make up for Sharon.

Chapter 9

The next morning, men and women gathered in their specific groups to start the festivities for the wedding. And as the day went on it was just beautiful to see people working together, everyone helping each other.

My father and mother arrived around 12:30 in the afternoon with the mayor, a priest and a camera man as Sharon had requested. And to my surprise my father also bought me a brand-new suit and some new shoes. That was when it all became real in my mind, I was getting married in a few hours.

By two o'clock in the afternoon the cooking was done, and the tables were set. Everybody was well dressed, and the traditional band singer was also ready to start the party. Now all we were waiting for was for Sharon to show up.

With my brand-new suit and black shoes on, I stood out by the roadside with confidence waiting for her to show up at any time. Still, I couldn't stop myself from thinking that she might not be able to escape, and the thought of it worried me. So, to stay optimistic I kept on going back to the last words she told me.

"Please do not give up on waiting for me no matter how long it takes, don't lose hope".

I repeated the same sentence over and over in my head trying to convince myself that she would make it. As three o'clock was fast approaching, I looked in every direction for a sign of her in vain. And just as the smallest noise from the bushes would call for my attention, so was even greater the sound of a car engine from a distance that made my heart beat twice as fast.

I was walking up and down the road every time I heard a car coming hoping it was Sharon, only to see the driver pass me by without paying any attention.

It was now 3:15 pm and still no sign of her, it felt like I had been waiting forever. My legs were getting tired from standing up, and with my brand-new shoes still tight, I could also feel my feet hurting. As time went on, with my already tired legs, despair started to grow in me every minute, and my concern for her safety became greater. I was now worrying for her wellbeing wondering if she escaped but took the wrong taxi. I was also questioning myself about the directions I gave her to find her way back to the village. Now in doubt, I could only pray to God for a miracle that she would appear from nowhere. Because all I wanted at that moment was to hear her voice to know that she was okay.

Then when I started to lose hope, even though she had asked me not to, a taxi stopped right in front of me. It was 3:30 pm, I looked through the passenger windows and there she was smiling. At last, not only I was relieved by her presence, but also my heart was full of joy to see her again. As soon as she got out of the taxi, we kissed, and she asked.

"Is everything ready for the wedding?"

"Yes, we were all waiting for you to start".

We walked into the courtyard to see everybody on their feet happily applauding to welcome her. With time pressing, my father and Uncle Konan gathered everybody to start the official wedding ceremony right away. After the Mayor certified the marriage license signed by Sharon and me, it was the priest's turn to make us recite our vows after him.

"Dieudonné Charles, do you take Sharon Johnson as your wife to cherish and to love forever, for better or worse until death do you part?"

"Yes, I do".

"And Sharon Johnson, do you take Dieudonné Charles as your husband to cherish and love forever, for better and worse until death do you part?"

"Yes, I do".

"I declare you husband and wife, and you may now kiss your bride".

We kissed with passion, and now legally married, we went right ahead without wasting any time to change our modern clothes to traditional African clothes, made by the village ladies for the traditional ceremony as Sharon requested.

Everything seemed to go so fast that I could barely recognize my new wife as she came out of the room a few minutes later. She was wearing a long handmade traditional cloth called Kente, made from cotton. Her Kente was dark blue with white stripes, tucked under her arms and covering her body from her chest to her knees.

She was beautiful and splendid with her make-up done by the village women. I was the happiest man in the world standing by her side, also dressed in the same cloth, but mine was a gold color with red stripes. My Kente was three times the size of Sharon's, it was as big as a king-sized blanket. The men helped me with my dress, as I put my cloth across my left shoulder, and it covered my entire body down to my feet.

The traditional band was playing in the background as we stood in front of Uncle Konan, the village chief, for the final wedding ceremony. As we were getting used to the sound of the music and happy atmosphere, suddenly the band stopped playing and the whole place became quiet. Curious of the unexpected silence, Sharon and I turned around, and to our surprise there were the two agents. They stood there silently about fifty feet away from us, perhaps wondering what was going on.

I could tell from the expression on their faces the frustration of what they might have gone through to get to the village with the blockade on the road. Although they looked upset, for some reason they didn't try to stop the ceremony, maybe out of respect or they were just overwhelmed by the number of people present. They waited until the ceremony was over, and Uncle Konan had given us his blessing. They walked calmly to Sharon and told her it was time to leave.

"I'm staying". She said.

Then she handed the marriage license to one of the agents in front of the mayor, and this time everybody was anxiously waiting to see the agents' reaction. After the agent read it, he shook his head in disbelief and told his partner.

"Our mission here is over, we can no longer force her to come with us".

He then handed the marriage license to his partner to read it himself.

"Congratulations". They both said. "We will let the Senator know about your decision".

As the agents were leaving without Sharon everybody started cheering and hugging one another. Sharon and I hugged and kissed, and it felt like a big weight lift off our back. And as I watched the two agents walk away, I realized Sharon was now free to stay as long as she would like. We both became more relaxed not having to worry anymore, and she could also now enjoy the wedding like a normal bride.

But to the surprise of everyone, my father and Uncle Konan walked up to the agents and asked them to be part of the celebration, to which they said. "No".
Then, Sharon also approached the agents to convince them to stay.

"Your presence will mean a lot to me. Being that I'm the only American, and you are the only other two present, it would be nice to have you be part of the celebration". She insisted.

They finally agreed to stay. And to think that a few minutes ago they were trying to take her away, and now here we were asking them to stay and be part of the celebration was a strange and happy feeling. The two agents were given a seat at the V.I.P table as honor guests, and the village chief ordered that food and drinks be served to them as they wished.

Contrary to what one would have thought about the villagers' reaction with respect to the agents, it was the complete opposite. The villagers used the opportunity to show their kindness and love to their guests and make them feel welcome. The agents sat at the V.I.P table in disbelief of the reception given to them by the village people, after all that happened the day before.

As the celebration went on, the agents became comfortable enough to accept an invitation on the dance floor. I could see the joy and the smiles on everyone's faces dancing with their partners, and that made the day even more special as Uncle Konan predicted.

I turned to my wife and said.
"You were right, dreams do come true if you believe in them, and today we are living proof".

Before the night was over the village chief offered a couple of rooms to the secret service agents, so that they could rest and safely travel the next day. And with the wedding now behind us I asked Sharon to tell me about her escape.

"I stayed in my room this morning after we had breakfast until lunch time to give the agents the impression that I was still tired from the trip. And after we had lunch at the hotel restaurant, I went back to my room again for a nap since our flight was at 5:30 pm. I waited for about fifteen minutes before escaping through my hotel room window. And I ran as fast as I could away from the hotel, and as soon as I got into the first taxi, I handed the driver the directions to the village you gave me".

"That was very courageous of you". I said.

"Do you know what kept me going while I was sitting in the taxi not knowing if I would make it to the village or not?"

"No".

"It was something you said to me on the terrace at the coffee place the second day after my arrival, about your parents having to make the decision to leave France with you for Africa".

"What did I say?" I asked.

You said. "You would be surprised how sometimes the circumstances in life make us take the unexpected decision for reasons that we can't explain, by doing so, making the hardest decision seems easy. So, as I was faced with the challenge of escaping for love, I found a courage within me that I didn't know existed before, and made me believe in myself, that I would make it to the village for the wedding no matter what happened".

I listened to her story with amazement as she told me her escape. And for her to remember my parent's story, and use it as a source of inspiration, I knew right there we were meant to be together.

The next morning as the agents were leaving, they thanked my father, the village chief and the villagers for their kindness and hospitality. They said good-bye to us and handed Sharon an envelope.

"This is a small wedding present from both of us, and we will forever remember your wedding". The agents said.

"Thank you and it means a lot to me that you were part of it". Sharon said.

Sharon opened the envelope and there was a one-hundred-dollar bill inside. And for the other agent to say.

"Sorry for what happened two days ago, we were just doing our job".

"I know". She said.

"You shouldn't be sorry for what you did two days ago". I said. "Because people in the village will always remember you for what you did yesterday, by being part of the wedding celebration. And as we say in Africa, if the end of the story is beautiful, so is the whole story".

We stayed in the village for another week for Sharon to finish her thesis, and finally the time came for us to say good-bye. Only this time the villagers also had the chance to say their good-bye by bringing Sharon a few gifts as souvenirs. They all gathered around my father's car with the children holding on to Sharon not wanting her to leave. It was a day filled with cries as we drove away.

We spent one more week with my parents in the city, as I prepared my passport to travel for the first time to the United States of America with my wife. It was easy for me to get a US visa, because of my French citizenship.

After Sharon's long conversation on the phone with her parents the night before our departure for the United States, I asked.

"How was their reaction to our marriage?"

"They were unhappy with me, because they were not expecting me to come to Africa and get married. But I'm sure they will like you when they get to know you". She replied quietly.

"Did you tell them that I was white?" I asked.

"No, I didn't". She replied.

"Why?" I asked.

"Because I thought after the surprise wedding, it would have been a little too much for them to take it all at once. I'd rather deal with the race part when we get there". She replied smiling.

"You know it's not funny, because I don't want to be blamed for everything". I said, and we both laughed.

Chapter 10

It was Saturday morning and once again another good-bye, only this time it was also me saying good-bye to my parents with Sharon at the airport. So here I was with my father at the same airport we welcomed Sharon to a little more than a month ago. But now with us was my mother and Uncle Konan, who came from the village the day before just to say good-bye to us. For the first time in my life, I was leaving my parents for another continent unknown to me, America. I hugged Uncle Konan, my mother, and my father good-bye with tears in my eyes. my father put his hands on both my shoulders and said with a smile.

"You will be okay son; may God be with you and your wife. Have a safe trip".

I was familiar with this way of talking from my father, his strong belief in God and asking for his blessing which reminded me sometimes of Uncle Konan. This was the African culture embodied in my father after living in Africa for more than twenty years. And like my father always said.

"Africa grows in you, and its culture becomes second nature".

My mother hugged me one last time and held me a little longer in her arms as if she would never see me again before we boarded the plane. So, for Sharon to remind her that it was just a good-bye because they would be coming to visit us the following year which brought a smile to all of us.

As we sat on the plane, we heard the captain's voice over the speaker welcoming the passengers. He gave us the flight itinerary and the arrival time, then asked us to fasten our seatbelt for a pleasant flight. I looked through the plane window one more time for a sign of my parents, unable to see anyone. I could only see my own reflection in the window glass and felt all alone. I was thinking of my parents and how much I missed them already, and I was also missing Africa, my home.

Then I heard the sound and the power of the engine underneath me shaking my seat as the plane taxied to the runway for takeoff. As the engine noise was getting louder, so was the vibration of my chair. Suddenly I was pushed back in my seat as the plane was leaving the runway, slowly climbing higher and higher in the air every second to find myself sitting in an awkward position. I could now see through my window laying halfway back, cars and houses on the ground getting smaller as everything slowly disappeared behind the clouds. After the plane settled at the correct altitude twenty minutes later, I felt Sharon squeezing my hand. That was when I realized she had been holding my hand through the whole takeoff, as to reassure me that I wasn't alone.

And every time that the plane gained in altitude, I felt my seat shaking and the whole plane moving left to right as if it was turbulence. I was afraid of heights, so being suspended in the air without any control, reminded me that I was on my own. I grabbed Sharon's hand each time there was turbulence to tell her that, if anything were to happen, we would be together. Nevertheless, I remained optimistic of any flights to arrive safely to their destination by telling myself that the captain, having studied hard to be a pilot, and followed diligent professional training would give his best for a safe flight, so he too, could be with his family. Eleven hours later, we heard the captain on a microphone.

"Ladies and gentlemen, as we prepare to land at New York International Airport, please fasten your seat belt, and make sure the backrest and folding trays are in an upright position. We wish you a nice stay in New York".

Soon after, all the passengers began applauding the captain for the beautiful landing. We walked inside the airport and to our surprise, there was a group of people waiting to welcome us, and a couple of journalists with their microphones for questioning. We learned then that the news in the US media was of a United States senator's daughter who went to Africa for research about African culture and ended up falling in love with an African man. It was a beautiful love story, and everyone wanted to know if it was true.

Sharon's parents were also waiting for us, but before the journalists could ask her any question, her father and his security were able to walk her away from the crowd to his car. I could tell from the excitement of her parents, that they were very happy to see her safe and sound.

"Where is Dieudonné?" Her father asked.

"Dad and mom, this is my husband, Dieudonné".

I was standing next to her with my suitcase in my hand, but no one paid any attention to me. I thought maybe because the airport was too crowded, her parents didn't notice me. But from the surprised look on her parents' faces after she introduced me to them as her husband, I realized they were expecting to see someone else, but me. Then I remembered, Sharon never told them about my race.

So as if her parents were not mad enough already about her unexpected marriage to someone from Africa, my race seemed to have made it even worse. Because the last thing they were expecting was their son-in-law from Africa to be white. I started to wonder, if all this time that I was standing there, they thought of me as an old friend she met on the plane.

Both of her parents stood there quietly for a few seconds next to the car in the parking lot. Her mother stared at me from head to toe and back, while her father looked at me straight in the eyes without saying a word as if I wasn't real. And suddenly out of nowhere he broke into a sarcastic laugh as if he couldn't believe what his daughter said, and what he was looking at. A bit awkward and confused about her parent's reaction toward me, I stood there calm and afraid, not knowing what to expect next. Then her father widely opened his arms to give me a big hug, and everybody started to laugh including me.

"Welcome to the family Dieudonné". Her father said with a big smile.

And me, I was just happy to hear him say my name. Then it was time for her mother to give me another hug.

"I told you not to worry too much about my parents". Sharon reminded me.

We arrived at her parents' house half an hour later, where her friends and family members were waiting to welcome us to a small reception. She introduced me to everyone, and after the reception she gave me a tour of the house. Her parents' house was a mansion made for a king compared to my parents' house in Africa. It was ten times bigger and hundred times more beautiful, each of the five bedrooms had its own big TV with a bathroom. There was a home theater in the basement with the most comfortable seats to find myself lost sitting in. Everything looked meticulously clean, and well organized as if it was put together by a professional home decorator. I was surprised when she told me her mother did everything.

The next day Sharon took me out for a tour of the city. New York was everything she told us about when she was in Africa. The buildings were big and tall, and seemed never-ending as if they were trying to reach the sky. The roads were wide, and the cars were driving next to each other bumper to bumper in traffic. I was walking on the streets of New York looking in every direction, and curious about every little thing. At times it felt as if I was dreaming, because twenty-four hours ago I was in Africa, and here I was for the first time in New York, the city where dreams are made.

I could also tell from my first impression that New York was different from France. It was vibrant and active. But New York compared to Africa was a different story, there were two worlds apart. In New York everybody seemed busy, and each person was minding his own business. But in Africa life was more relaxed, and people did things at their own pace. You could talk to someone on the street in Africa without knowing them and tell a joke as if you were old friends. You could even invite yourself into a conversation without knowing the people, and it was all in good faith and fun to start a friendly conversation.

We went to Central Park, and it was exactly as Sharon described it in her letter. The place was full of people walking with their dogs, running, and biking. In some areas of the park, the trees were big enough to remind me of Africa, and for a moment it felt like being back home.

We went to McDonald's at noon for lunch. I ordered the biggest Hamburger on the menu, which I had always dreamed of. The hamburger had a slice of onion, tomato, with some salad, one on top of each other. The whole thing was on top of a piece of melting cheese and some grilled meat patty, between two bums of white bread. With some French fries and a large cold glass of Coca Cola. The Hamburger was as beautiful to look at as it was tasty to eat, with each bite going through my mouth, it felt like I was in heaven. After a delicious lunch, and a beautiful day filled with new discoveries, we returned home to her parents.

We stayed with her parents, and as the weeks went on, her father became more receptive to our marriage, contrary to her mother who was still reluctant. I had the feeling that she thought I married her daughter for reasons other than love. But I understood where she was coming from, she was a concerned and loving mother who wanted the best for her daughter, and didn't want to see her get hurt. So, day by day I got used to her mother's reluctance, and I prayed that God would give her the chance to get to know me. Because after all, only Sharon and I knew the love we had for each other, and it was the only thing that mattered to us.

Chapter 11

A month later it was Sharon's turn for her graduation ceremony. She was standing in line in her shiny blue gown with a group of graduate students to receive her master's degree in African studies. At the end of the graduation ceremony, her parents, friends, family members and I congratulated her. Then we all drove home for the graduation party.

But before the party could start, to the surprise of everybody except me, Sharon invited all of us to the theater room in the basement, where she had something special planned in advance. As we all sat down in the comfortable seats with some people standing up in the back of the room, she stood in front of the big white movie screen to give the most beautiful speech I had ever heard.

"I would like to tell my parents, and everyone present here today something special. But I will start first by saying thank you to my parents for making this day possible. Thank you, mom, and dad, for your love and your support. Thank you to my husband, for your love and all your help with my research. And thank you to all of you for being here to celebrate with me.

"Since I came back from Africa, I planned for this special moment with my husband.
So, I would ask you to please bear with me for the next twenty minutes, for me to share with you my story, and what I learned about Africa during those six weeks that changed my life for the best.

"I went to Africa to do my thesis for my master's degree in African studies, about life and culture in Africa. Although, I have always thought of myself to be an open-minded person, someone who wanted to discover new things and learn about other cultures. Still in the back of my mind, my ego made me believe that I would be the one teaching something to the village people. But boy, was I wrong. Little did I know, I would be the one getting a life lesson.

"Everything I learned about Africa in school was like night and day compared to my experience among the village people. And all the things I took for granted through my entire life growing up in America, Africa gave me a new perspective. Because I never wondered once in my life how much labor went into farming before the food got to my table. But it took me only a week helping on the farm, spending time with a farmer to understand how hard he had to work to feed his family. The family most of the time ate the same food every day without complaining. And for me to remember how many choices of food I had in America. I had so many choices that sometimes, I couldn't decide what I wanted for dinner or remember what I had for lunch six hours earlier. After my experience at the farm, I'm today thankful to see food on my table, and grateful to whomever cooked it.

"Water, which is so simple, but vital to life, in the village, it took hard work to get. The women would go to the well early in the morning and late in the afternoon to get the water for daily use. The morning water was used for cooking and drinking. The drinking water was poured into a big ceramic handmade jar, and then the jar was put on top of a large flat bowl filled with wet sand to keep the water cold. When in the city all it took for a glass of water was just a turn of the faucet and a refrigerator. The afternoon water was for showering, where the children took a cold shower every night, and only the parents took a hot shower. All of this reminded me of those long hot showers I used to take without asking myself where the water came from.

"When it came to work in the village, the men did the hard work at the farm to take care of their families, and the women were responsible of the household and the children. Everyone was happy to do their share of work without complaint and proud to be a family. But above all, one of the most amazing things for me was to see neighbors helping neighbors, watching after all children as their own, and sometimes the whole village gathering to help a family in crisis.

"The village people were not educated nor were they rich. But they were the most kind and welcoming people I have ever met in my life. Although they didn't have much to give, they were still willing to share the little that they had with a stranger, because their belief in God was greater than anything. They believed that, if they were kind to a stranger and grateful even to the youngest among them, God would bless them and their children.

"Their entire lives revolved around their families, their farms, their faith, and the community. But what kept the family strong, and the community together was the first traditional rule they all live by, respect for their elders. Whether man or woman, all the villagers carried the same respectful attitude toward their elders and the rest of the community, for the birthright is a sign of wisdom. Because they knew respect-built character, and character is what makes a man".

"This was my story and how much I learned about life from the people that I expected the least from a small village in Africa. This experience has humbled me and made me appreciate today, all the things I took for granted yesterday, and has changed my life to be a better person. It also taught me that one doesn't know everything in life. Because we never stop learning. Now you understand why I said earlier that I was the one who ended up getting a life lesson from the village people".

After everybody stopped clapping for her beautiful speech. She said.

"Now to conclude I would like to show the final surprise, our wedding video".

It was a big surprise to everyone in the room, especially to her parents who didn't even know that a video of our wedding existed. As we all watched the video with excitement for the first time on the big screen, I could not have predicted how much her parents would have been touched by it. Her mother couldn't retain her tears, while her father sat there quietly watching the video with all his attention. He smiled from time to time as if he was there at the wedding. I guess her parents were just amazed to see how beautiful and happy she looked in the video. At the end of the video everyone in the room had tears in their eyes. Sharon's mother walked over to her and gave her a big hug, and standing next to her, she said in a soft voice.

"Before everyone present here, I would like to say a few words to my daughter and my son-in-law, Dieudonné".

Surprised and unexpected, I was happy to hear her call me her son-in-law. But I was also nervous sitting in my chair not knowing what she would say.

"Dieudonné, I'm sorry, because I have always believed that you married my daughter so you could come to the United States for a green card. But after watching your wedding video, I realized I was wrong all along. I doubted your love for Sharon, but now I'm more convinced than ever it was love that brought you both together, and I'm happy to have you in our family. It was a beautiful wedding and I wish we could have been there, thank you".

After hearing those beautiful words, I walked to my mother-in-law and gave her a hug.

"Let's start the party". Sharon said.

It was a beautiful graduation party; everybody was happy and danced through the night. And for me it was the best day of my life in America, because I had been waiting for that day of acceptance from her mother since my arrival in America.

A few days later Sharon and I, with her parents as witnesses went to the city office to get a marriage license to legalize our marriage in the United States. Because for me to get a temporary green card and be able to legally work in the United States, we needed to be married on American soil. And after the official ceremony was over, we had a small private dinner at a restaurant.

"I have an announcement". Sharon said to her parents during dinner.

Both her parents anxiously looked at her as if to expect the news of a newborn.

It's not what you are thinking". She said smiling. "Dieudonné and I have decided to have a big party next summer to celebrate with everybody our one-year anniversary where you will get to meet Dieudonné's parents who are flying from Africa to visit".

Her parents could not have been happier of the news to be part of the celebration next time around. A week later we moved out of her parents' house and rented an apartment in

Brooklyn. For the first time of our marriage, we were living on our own and we felt like a true married couple. Sharon spent the rest of her time turning her thesis into a book about her life experience in Africa, which was published and became a bestseller, titled. "The Life and Culture in Africa ".

After a little more than two months of married life and living together in the United States, I was once again a student, now taking English as a second language at a nearby university looking for a new career path in computer science.

One afternoon with Sharon still at work, I was sitting in the living room, listening to some African music. All alone and homesick, I found myself at last reflecting on the past. I wondered which one of us in their wildest dream would have thought, that a simple correspondence through writing could have ended up being the best love story of our lives?
I remembered not too long ago, when we first met and were surprised by the color of our skin. And I learned that night how she felt about getting married to someone of a different race.

A little bit disappointed, with lost hope, I left things to time. And as time went on, we overcame our differences and learned that we had more in common. We learned that like everything else in life, when confronted with a challenge. The same way our mind helps us find a solution to a problem, so does our heart for challenges of love. Because the solution to our race was always within us, in our heart. All we needed to do was to listen to the voice in our heart to guide us. And after we did just that, our heart helped us cross the racial barrier, and slowly brought us close together to set us on the path for love.

Then we understood that, even if love is blind, it could still see love in the other person's heart. And although love has no boundary, it will always have many obstacles to conquer to find its other half. But it will take two hearts loving each other to overcome barriers, and in the end, love will always win. Because love is kind, love is patient and love is forgiven, for it is the most powerful and beautiful thing that we have within us.

End.